# A Heart for Hubris

Cathy Smith

Published by Cathy Smith, 2018.

A HEART FOR HUBRIS

**First edition. March 14, 2018.**

Copyright © 2018 Cathy Smith.

ISBN: 979-8230042938

Written by Cathy Smith.

# Table of Contents

# Cupid's Intrigue

THE LEAD TABLET PLEASED Nemesis. People inscribed curses and chanted them in black magic rituals to invoke her. This lament from a scorned lover came to her along fumes of acrid musk.

She chuckled her appreciation over the verse, savoring the rage in each meter. The Muses's insipid music at Olympus's feasts couldn't compare to this.

*I'll need two arrows.* She thought to herself as she looked over her armory, searching for a fitting tool to answer this lament. *One to shoot the one who scorned them, and the other for my petitioner if I like the look of them.*

She cursed when she saw her quiver was empty. Cupid's servant Zephyr delivered them once a month. He wasn't due for another two weeks, so she'd have to pick them up herself.

Cupid forged the arrows from special alloys that compelled or repelled love. Hephaestus could've object to this but didn't. Cupid's talent for forging his own weapons gave Hephaestus hope his wife's boy was his son. Allowing Cupid to keep this hobby helped him maintain this belief.

Cupid also forged the golden apples his mother granted to her favorites, "It must be nice to have a hobby. I only got to weave Jocasta a girdle before Athena complained to the Fates," Venus said when she saw the first apple.

Sometimes Cupid's mother wanted to see unseemly passions incited out of spite. Cupid delegated such missions to Nemesis and gave her a supply of love arrows to carry them out. He always gave her more than she needed but didn't like it when she used them up too fast on her personal pursuits.

ALL THE OLYMPIANS HAD grandiose castles, but Cupid had the best taste. He collected souvenirs of his wanderings and had a gallery of the choicest objets d'art. They got ogled as if they were nymphs.

He was admiring his newest possession when Nemesis came into his presence. Cupid held up a cameo of an exquisite young woman. She could've been a nymph were she not fully clothed like any maiden from a respectable family.

"Do you think the artist had a live model to work from?" He sighed at the question.

"If not then you can get your mother to breathe life into her like she did to Galatea," Nemesis murmured. "Hephaestus could help you if she doesn't."

"Hephaestus's statues are anatomically correct, but Mother's work is more lifelike. I don't want a moving doll."

Nemesis laughed, "You sound like you got pricked by your own arrows."

He sighed at this, and it seemed a good time to make her petition, "Do you have any more arrows I can use?" She unslung her quiver to show it was empty.

He grimaced, "I gave you a fresh batch of arrows two weeks ago, along with my list."

She sniffed, "Do you expect me to do your dirty work without fair compensation, Cupid? You're lucky I haven't demanded your favors in trade once you came of age."

He frowned, "I'll give you five extra above the assigned equipment tally to use at your discretion." He made a wave and invisible hands blew arrows into the empty quiver.

"I want 10 extra a month," she said.

He glanced at her. "You can't be so desperate for companionship that you need so many aids?"

She gritted her teeth. "I hate the thought of taking off my body armor and disguising myself as a nymph,"

He chuckled. "It's no worse than the shapechanges other Olympians use in the pursuit of love… "

SHE'D FLOUNCED OUT but regretted it the next month. There was no way her allotment would last a month without her nymph disguise.

She reserved 10 for her personal use regardless of the number of assignments on the new list. When she saw there was 15 arrows left, she went over her list to see which ones she'd cover.

Her eyebrows rose over a charge of blasphemy from Venus. Venus had charged no one with blasphemy before. It contained a rolled-up sketch of that lovely girl from Cupid's cameo. *Psyche of Corinth, has usurped the worship that's my due. Her images are in my shrines...*

Nemesis smirked at this.

SHE MARCHED BACK TO Cupid's mansion with the scroll in hand. He was practicing his aim in the back with a target range. His skill would've been formidable if his arrows were meant to kill.

"What is it?" He asked.

"Did you have the chance to look this over?" she asked.

He grunted, "I pretty much know a letter sealed with a black wax by mother is a hit job. I don't bother."

"Well you should," she unrolled the scroll to show Psyche's sketch.

His eyes widened.

"This is the target, Psyche of Corinth. Venus wants her to fall in love with a human monster since her images are now in your mother's shrines."

He frowned. "The cameo was a part of the parcels delivered to me. I thought it was a present."

He grabbed the scroll out of her hand, "Let me deal with this."

*Maybe this will be the last time Cupid delegates his hit jobs to me,* Nemesis mused.

She'd miss the arrows.

IT WAS HARD TO TELL if Cupid would stop outsourcing his dirty work to her or not. She didn't see Cupid for over two weeks, but he could've found some new bauble to delight himself with. He had the instincts of a magpie when he saw something pretty and shiny.

She would know for sure at the next banquet. It was the only way to get her allotment of ambrosia and Dionysus's wine. Otherwise, she'd avoid it since the regular menu was too sweet for her taste.

Cupid came for the confections the pastry chef made. Nemesis noticed he lost his appetite when Venus asked, "Has anyone seen Psyche of Corinth?"

"Psyche of Corinth?" Hera asked.

"She's the one who usurped my worship with her images," Venus sniffed. "No one's seen her in weeks."

Cupid laughed, "Isn't that what you wanted, Mother? For her memory to fade?"

"But she isn't in Tartarus! I checked with Proserpine, and she's not in the Underworld," Venus sniffed.

"Tartarus?" Juno shrieked, "And you say I'm vindictive when I'm scorned."

Venus flushed red at this while Minerva raised an eyebrow, "It sounds extreme."

"You didn't begrudge Helen of Troy her day in the sun, Mother. Why shouldn't Psyche of Corinth have hers?" Cupid asked.

"Helen of Troy was a daughter of Zeus, a demi-goddess, not a mere mortal!"

Mars laughed. "Maybe Psyche of Corinth got carried off like the Sabean Women did? She'd make a marvelous war trophy."

Venus glared at him.

He sighed, "Put a bounty on her if you can't find her. That's what I'd do."

Nemesis watched Cupid all the while. He took a big gulp out of his goblet at Mars' suggestion.

CUPID PRACTICED HIS archery whenever he was upset. Nemesis joined him at the range after the banquet. "You know where Psyche of Corinth is don't you?"

He shot a bull's eye. She took a shot and split his arrow, "You wouldn't be the first Olympian to carry off a mortal."

"How much will it cost to keep this between us, Nemesis?"

"I want 10 arrows a month," she said.

He nodded and then walked off the range.

OLYMPUS THOUGHT THE extra arrows were Nemesis's compensation for Cupid's dirty work. Venus thought Cupid should trade his own favors instead, but Nemesis said, "Your son is too soft for my taste."

Yet, Zephyr sent her a letter summoning her to Venus's palace. The scroll was in Cupid's handwriting, so she came. Cupid lay on a couch with a bandage around his right wing. "Tell people you got rough with me if anyone asks."

"Huh?"

"Tell Olympus we were together to explain the burn on my wing."

She snorted, "A burn on your wing? I've had rougher sessions with mortals. Don't tell me Psyche played rough with you?"

"Her pregnancy has made her lonely and moody, so I let her sisters come to visit her. Their sneers made her want to see who the father of her child was, and some oil spilled from the lamp while I slept."

"Humph. It's not as if you're Hephaestus. Why hide yourself?"

They both heard footsteps and a sniff. Venus walked into the room and gave a snort when she glanced at Nemesis. "Stay away from my son, you harpy!"

"It was a onetime experiment. It'll never happen again," Cupid said.

"The least you can do is cover for him while he recovers," Venus said.

Nemesis sighed, realizing there'd be more work to keep up this fiction than she thought. Venus would get her thrown to Tartarus if she refused to make her supposed amends. She shook her head but said nothing to contradict Venus's assumptions.

Cupid stood up from the couch. "I better give her my list and arrows," he said as a pretext to speak to Nemesis in private.

"I'll get them," Venus said, pushing her son back down onto the couch.

"No, I can do it."

"I don't want you moving from the couch."

"I'll have Zephyr send them over," Cupid said.

Venus's eyes narrowed. She knew all the signs of mischief from Cupid's childhood. "No, I'm going over to your home myself. I want to see what you're up to."

Cupid gave a deep sigh.

Nemesis sniffed at the spectacle of his cowardice. *Definitely too soft for my liking.*

"You could've saved yourself trouble by telling her a better lie," she sighed.

"Like what?"

"You could've said a spark flew up from your forge and landed on your wing."

Cupid slapped his forehead when he heard this.

Venus came back into the room with a quiver full of arrows and handed them to Nemesis. She turned to face her son, "I want you to know I cleared out the trash in your palace."

Cupid winced as Venus flounced out.

He gripped Nemesis shoulder, "Find Psyche for me and get her to a shelter. She shouldn't be out in the open in her condition."

Nemesis frowned at this, and he smirked, "So you're no better than me. You don't want to risk my mother's wrath either."

She gritted her teeth at this. "I will give Psyche what help I can, but not openly."

THE PROMISE WAS MADE though there was no telling if Psyche was still living. Psyche was a pregnant mortal, and a fall from Olympus wasn't good for her health.

The first thing she did was talk to Zephyr. She went to Cupid's doorstep, "Zephyr, I'm performing Cupid's duties as he recovers at his mother's place. Did you see what happened to Psyche of Corinth?"

Zephyr was ever attentive to the God and Goddess of Love and came when they called. He knew Cupid outsourced unpleasant tasks to her and answered her question. "Venus would've had me dash Psyche's brains against the cliffs if she didn't see she was pregnant. I set her down the public highway on Venus's orders instead."

"Show me where you left her."

He propelled her to Psyche's location since he was invisible and couldn't show her any other way. When the windstorm ended she saw nearby vultures circling a particularly succulent morsel.

Nemesis became an eagle and saw the maiden eye the offerings on roadside altar to Ceres. She looked like she wanted to eat them but cleaned up the roadside alter instead.

Nemesis heard the prayer when Zephyr wafted it up to her. "Could I please have something to eat, Ceres?"

"I am sorry, Psyche. I dare not anger Venus by helping you," was the reply.

Nemesis sighed. *It seems I'm no better. I won't openly oppose Venus either, but there are ways to work my purpose.*

Zephyr conveyed her words to Venus. "I see Psyche of Corinth before me. Do you wish me to strike her down for hubris now or after the child's birth?"

The question could've been from any petitioner.

She heard a sigh on the wind, "After."

"There won't be an 'after' if Psyche and the babe she carries perish from hunger first," she muttered.

Another sigh came on the wind. "Bring her to my nearest temple, so she can have food and lodging."

Nemesis shifted into the shape of a fluffy dove and alighted on the shrine, giving an insipid coo.

Psyche gasped, "Are you from Cupid?"

She gave another coo, bobbed her head 'yes', and fluttered her wings priming Psyche to follow her when she took off.

The temple was little better than a hostel. Nemesis didn't like the assessing look the priest gave Psyche. Psyche was still beautiful though heavy with the baby. His words confirmed Nemesis's misgivings, "The pilgrims will like to see a new girl. It'll mean more offerings."

Psyche sighed, her eyes downcast, but she entered the temple.

Nemesis assumed her own form and Zephyr relayed her words to Venus. "Are you sure Psyche will be suitable for temple work in her condition?"

A huff fluttered its way to the air along Zephyr's currents. "Well she must make herself useful somehow."

Zephyr moved to deliver Venus's words to the priest's ear. He was past the age for Venus's favors, but familiar with her voice.

"We'll wait until you deliver to put you into service. You can sort the grain offerings in the meantime," he said to Psyche.

Psyche nodded at this.

There was a tinkle of malicious laughter from the air. "You must sort the whole room to earn your keep tonight."

Psyche's face fell and Nemesis cursed. She landed on the ground, to speak to the ants she used to ravage the impious's crops.

"Food!" the tiny voices cackled.

"Tell Psyche you'll sort the grains in the Temple's grainery if she sets aside a part of her supper for you."

They said, "We will obey."

Nemesis sighed, "I've done all I can for her this day. I've got other duties I must attend to."

SHE FINISHED THE DAY'S duties and went back to see how Cupid fared. Skin had grown over the burn but the dander wasn't back yet. When she gave her report on Psyche, she got a quiverful of love arrows for her own use.

She also received a list of targets and the commission to continue to protecting Psyche. Nemesis assumed Psyche was safe enough for the night. That's why she waited to check on her during her morning flight. She carried herself on swift and strong eagle's wings to get a good overview of the land. Psyche was trekking towards a mountain.

She landed next to Psyche. "What do you think you're doing wandering about in your condition?"

Psyche sobbed with weariness and fear, "I have to fetch a cup of water from the spring at the top of this mountain."

"Nnnn. Sit down in that shade over there and wait until I come back," she gripped the cup in her beak and flew up to the spring.

She filled the cup and flew back to Psyche. Psyche cried in either gratitude or because her pregnancy made her tearful. The mortal took the cup from her in shaking hands.

"Don't drop it because I won't go up for you again. I've got other things to do before the day is over!"

Nemesis went back to Cupid, hoping he'd be well enough to take on his duties and his mortal wife's cause.

THERE WAS A LIST WAITING for her when she went to see Cupid. It was the only reason Venus's household staff let her in.

He was flexing his wings to ease them out of their stiffness. "You need to get back ASAP, Cupid. Your mother is getting creative with the labors she gives Psyche."

Cupid frowned, "Labors?"

"I saved her a journey to a steep mountain top. That's a herculean task for a pregnant woman."

"I need another day," Cupid said. "Check on her for me tomorrow."

Nemesis snorted at this, and she got another 10 love arrows as pre-payment for her work.

SHE CHECKED FOR PSYCHE at midday. This time Psyche was at a riverbank. She looked across it to a grove filled with sheep; they had golden fleece, sharp horns, teeth, and hooves. Psyche sobbed at the sight of them.

*What is it now?*

She landed next to her, shifting from an eagle to a woman.

"I—I've got to gather their wool," she pointed to ram whose baas sounded more like bellows.

"I know a trick to collecting the wool if you'll pay me with the coin of love," a masculine voice said.

Psyche started. She couldn't tell where the voice came from and was aghast at the suggestion.

Nemesis snorted at this, "The God of Love has claimed this woman for himself. Her favors aren't available for trade, River God."

Nemesis took out a golden arrow of love. "I offer you this. You can use it against the next target of your choice."

She dropped the arrow in the water. "The sheep take naps in the trees' shade the afternoon. You can cross me safely then. You can pick as much wool as you need from the bushes and trees while they sleep. Then you must cross back before they awake, or they'll swarm you."

He paused, "Give me an arrow every time you cross over, and I'll slow down the rapids for you."

Nemesis grunted and took two arrows out and gave them to Psyche, "You heard him, now hear me. Use these to pay your toll, but don't touch the tips, or you'll fall in love with whomever you see. I've got errands to run and don't have time for this."

ANOTHER DAY CAME WITH another list. Nemesis was so busy she didn't check on Psyche until mid-afternoon. She was flying about as an eagle and gave a swift glance in the mortal's direction. Psyche was peering out the ledge of a high tower.

"What do you think you're doing?" She screeched when she landed on the edge.

"Venus wants her favorite beauty cream from Proserpine. I don't know how to get there, but this seemed the quickest way to Tartarus," she said.

Nemesis glanced down. "That it is, mortal, but the trick's getting back out of Tartarus again."

Psyche sobbed.

"Stop that! There's no need to blubber! I know of a quick entrance. I go there to witness against souls they send to Tartarus."

Psyche sobbed all the harder.

"What I'm trying to say is I can show you a cave that'll give you a fast way in and out if you're on godly business."

OF COURSE, THEY HAD to get Psyche down to the cave first. Venus told her the task had to be done in time for her to prepare for a dinner with the gods that evening. Psyche had used up the morning climbing the tower and Nemesis had to fly her down in eagle form to the cave.

Nemesis had a rope on her person in case she had to lash down any of her charges. She knotted up a harness around Psyche but didn't like the way it wrapped around her growing belly. Nemesis constructed a loose harness for herself, so Psyche had reins to hold onto for the flight.

When they landed and her passenger got off Nemesis muttered. "You'll must pay a toll to two gatekeepers in Tartarus.

Here are two silver dinars for Charon the ferryman. Give him one each for your forward and return journeys.

When you land on the riverbank, the most well-kept road will be to Pluto and Proserpine's palace; follow it.

At their gate you'll you will see the three-headed dog Cerberus—"

Psyche shuddered.

"The trick to passing him is to give him one piece of meat for each mouth. Otherwise, you must rush past him, which is impossible for you now. Heroes make trouble for themselves when they only give him one piece of meat. I'll catch you six small game animals to give to him, so you can enter and exit the palace."

She took a pouch and canteen on her waist and frowned, "I better give you my lunch too, and catch an extra rabbit for myself. Proserpine will have a feast laid out on a table and offer it to you. You must eat none of the food from the Underworld or you'll get trapped there."

Lastly, she placed a love arrow in Psyche's hand, "Give this to Proserpine if she demands payment for her cream. Venus may have an account she's neglecting, and Proserpine won't let a mortal take the cream on credit."

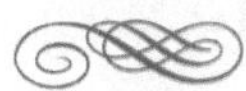

NEMESIS FINISHED HER errands before she came back to see Cupid. "No more lists! It's bad enough I have to do your work and my own but shielding a mortal from your mother's wrath is too much. Especially when she sent her to Tartarus to collect her favorite beauty cream."

Cupid's radiance became less rosy. "Mother, doesn't have a favorite cream. She uses a draught that gives her beauty sleep!"

At least it got him off his couch, Nemesis had to show him where she left Psyche. They found Psyche lying prone on the ground.

Cupid sucked the draught out of Psyche with a kiss on her mouth, and she awoke. "Cupid!"

*Young love!* Nemesis almost sneered. It'd be touching if it'd last, but she couldn't see it happening with Cupid being such a mama's boy.

She snorted, "You're better off letting her go rather than allow your mother to abuse her like this."

Psyche gasped, touched her bulging stomach and sobbed. Nemesis rolled her eyes, "Your arrows and her looks could guarantee her a good match, Cupid. Give this baby a stepfather if you won't be a proper husband to Psyche."

Psyche laughed bitterly at this, "People came to see me, but men were too awed to offer me marriage."

"Humph," Nemesis gave Cupid a hard look that dimmed his rosy radiance. "Venus is the Goddess of Love, and she gets men hot. They can't keep their hands off her."

Psyche frowned at this. Nemesis continued, "Did you keep the men away, so you could keep Psyche to yourself, Cupid?"

Cupid's mouth hardened, "I'm the God of Love. I'm the last one who should be sexless."

"If you can inhibit a beauty's natural sex appeal use it as leverage. Zeus could blast you, but he can't stand to live without what you provide. You can horrify Venus with a bout of celibacy..."

All Olympus grumbled at Nemesis for giving Cupid "ideas." They celebrated Psyche and Cupid's union with a toast of ambrosia to stop him from having more of them. Psyche and Cupid's daughter Voluptas was born three months later.

Thus, Psyche escaped the charge of hubris though Nemesis was still involved in her case.

# The Ambrosian Mysteries

MY NAME IS AMBROSIA, daughter of Ambrose Sanctus. I assumed Mother was Tia, a former vestal virgin though I found out differently later.

Despite my ignorance of Mother's true lineage, she was ever present in my childhood. She taught me how to read and write scrolls. That's why I can write about the Ambrosian Mysteries for the public record. I never thought I'd be writing a sacred text. Writing is only used to keep accounts in our household, so this scroll will lack finesse. I don't think Mother ever wanted to do more than that with her scrolls. Either out of lack of interest or to make sure she didn't frighten Father with her learning.

I would've had no reason to complain if I was only the patrician's daughter I thought I was at first. Father suspected Mother came from an Imperial line. He assumed her service at a vestal shrine freed her from her father's authority. Most patricians give their daughters to the shrine if they're unmarriageable. Some girls are too poor for proper dowries. There's also those, so uncomely they'd remain virgins either way. Why not make a civic virtue out of necessity?

I love Mother, but it must've been obvious she'd grow to be an Amazon in her early youth. Men prefer their women be dryads. Mother is well-made, but the dryad of an oak, and I take after her.

At least her family saw she was well provided for. When her term of service ended she retired in the province of Arcadia. Vestal virgins are emancipated from their father's authority. This meant she didn't need his approval to marry her neighbor.

Vestal virgins serve for 30 years and are then released with a modest pension. They are "allowed to marry" after their term, but there're few men who want an older bride.

"Your mother was old for a bride but young for a wife," Father says when he talks of their courtship.

I didn't understand what he meant at first. Eventually I understood there were matrons who maintained their looks and their households. They were beautiful. Yet it would be a disgrace to be never married at their advanced ages. It was better to be widowed or divorced.

Our frequent visitors gave me a glimpse of this world. Every time there was a shower a woman with a scandalously short chifton appeared. I assumed Iris was an athlete who spent most of her time in the gymnasium. That would explain why she saw no reason to wear anything but exercise clothes outside it.

She had the lean body and quick movements you'd expect of a circus performer. Mother served her light refreshments when she visited. They spoke of household matters that bored me when I was a child. I barely paid attention to what they gossiped about. Iris loved sweets. Mother always gave her fresh grape juice in a wineskin and an almond and raisin mix in a pouch before she went on her way.

There was also a man who came about the place with scrolls who got similar treatment. Mother would read the scrolls and sign or make her own notes. Our neighbors were scandalized she received the messenger herself. They assumed Father was naïve to think the man was nothing more than a courier what with the short toga he wore.

Mother never gave Father cause to doubt her loyalties. Though he may've been too in awe of her obvious breeding to object if her eye wandered. "I can't help looking at your mother and thinking 'this must be what Juno looks like.'"

It's a good thing for Mother, Father is no Jupiter, "I've only got so much energy. It's either use it to keep watch over my herds or to chase women."

His friends told him he would've been better off marrying a maiden who could bear him more children. "You need a younger bride to give you a proper namesake." For Father is Ambrose while I am Ambrosia.

Mother has the same tastes as him, and they make a good team. They gave me a pleasant childhood even if I chafed from the boredom at times.

Mother was generous, but her gifts were rustic, so it took a while to appreciate the golden bough she gave me. She'd presented me a golden bough full of ripe fruit that became my orchard on my 13th birthday. It shone like the purest gold, and I asked, "What goldsmith made this? Is it for my dowry?"

I assumed this was an ornate art piece meant for my future home. Mother frowned. She didn't like it when my nursemaid Charis told her I'd be of marriageable age soon. "You're too young to be thinking of marriage, Ambrosia."

"Charis says I shouldn't wait as long as you did to get married," I said.

"A maiden shouldn't get married until she's finished growing," she sniffed in distaste. "Diana wouldn't need to be placated at weddings if maidens weren't married so young. She doesn't want women to be maidens all their lives, but she thinks they are taken from her protection too soon."

I gaped at her. Charis expected me to be married off when my first blood moon came, "How do you know this?"

There was a long period of silence until she gave a loud sigh. "It is one of the mysteries I learned during my years of service."

"Oh," I said, assuming this was nothing more than piety on her part.

I looked at her. "I don't think I want to wait as long as you did."

She sighed. "We'll see what happens, Little One. In the meantime, you'll have extra time to amass a dowry."

I glanced at the golden bough, happy to change the subject, "So the goldsmith can make me more jewels?"

She laughed at this, "This bough isn't dead metal. It's a living plant."

"Did he plate it with gold?"

"No, you can still eat it," she plucked an apple from a branch to prove it and handed it to me.

I hefted it in my hand. It was heavy, but with life juices instead of gold. I brought it to my nose and inhaled a glorious bouquet as satisfying as Father's vintages. I was allowed to sip them before they fermented. My mouth watered, and I licked its skin, which was as sweet as honey.

"That's it," Mother said. "Bite it."

I did so. It was like a honeycake made by our chef, but it needed no honey to sweeten it.

"These golden apples are good, Mother. We ought to graft the bough to some roots in the orchard and transplant it," I said.

Mother smiled at this, and I understood the reason she'd given me this golden bough. She wanted me to become as fond of farming as she and father were.

GROWING THAT GOLDEN bough took over all my free time. Father looked at it and said, "I don't think we have roots deep enough to hold that bough."

That's why I grafted the branches that were little more than twigs to sapling roots. This left me with a stout bough with branches that were too thick and stiff to prune. I assumed it would die because none of the young saplings could hold it. Then I remembered my old treehouse in our gnarliest and oldest tree. Its top branches were becoming dry and hollow, and Father had told me, "It's about to die."

The same could be said for the golden bough itself, so why not give both as much time as I could?

A non-living branch of the old tree was sawed off until only the barely living stump remained. The golden bough was grafted by whittling it in a shape to fit the stump. I wrapped it with linen strips from Mother's loom to keep it in place until it grew into the stump.

THE NEXT DAY A GOLDEN tinge had drifted from the bough to rest of the tree. I took Mother and Father on a walk in the orchard, "Is it supposed to be like this?"

Father touched the golden sheen. "It's acting more like a rust than it is a graft."

Mother looked upon it with a frown, "The golden bough is fighting for its life."

"Like a fungus on its host?" I asked remembering past dinner conversations my parents had.

"It's a pretty fungus at least," Father said.

Mother sighed, "It's not shortening the apple tree's life by too much even if it's acting like a fungus. It was already dying. Let's see what happens."

I spent all my free time in the orchard then. Watching the golden bough fungi spread itself was more fun than playing with dolls.

WHEN FATHER'S BIRTHDAY came Mother gave him a lamb with a golden fleece. "You shouldn't have sprinkled gold dust on its coat. It can't be good for the poor thing."

He touched it to see if it was still healthy and gave a yelp when it bit him. I gasped when I saw it drew blood. "It must be a ram." He laughed.

"The gold dust must make it testy," I said.

"Perhaps, I should take it down to the spring to wash it?" he asked.

"I hope it washes off! Or else the poor thing will be pushed out of the flock like poor Blackie," I said.

Blackie was our black sheep. A lively, little ewe lamb I kept as a pet since her wool was unsalable. We were going to fatten her up for the table at first, but I couldn't stand the thought of doing so then.

"We'll see," Father said.

WASHING GOLDIE'S COAT caused it to shine like the sun. The other sheep squealed in terror at the sight of it. The flock was too afraid to touch him.

Father patted Goldie on the head. "I don't know if Blackie will accept a fellow misfit. She might follow the way of the flock and shun him, but maybe she'll enjoy the company."

So, Father's gift was put into Blackie's pen. Blackie shuddered at the sight of another sheep. We'd had to keep her separated from the flock since birth. The few times she'd been around the rest of the flock hadn't been good for her. Blackie squealed at the sight of Goldie, too petrified to move away when he came closer. He pressed his muzzle next to hers. Their muzzles touched for several moments but at least they weren't biting each other.

When it came time for their dinner, they fed at opposite ends of the trough. We left them in the pen like that.

WHEN WE TOLD MOTHER what happened among the flock she muttered, "So he's with Blackie? I never thought of that."

"Huh?"

"It never occurred to me Goldie wouldn't be accepted by the flock because he's as odd to them as a black sheep is," she said.

I visited the pen each morning. Within a month Blackie and Goldie were side-by-side. It was too bad this first happened in the orchard where I planted my golden bough transplants.

I had set up the golden bough saplings in their own section and went to check on them each morning. One day I saw Blackie and Goldie there grazing on the saplings, "No, shoo!"

I ran to get a shepherd's crook to push them away while they nibbled on the saplings. They kept on munching all the while. By the time I came back the saplings were gone, and they'd eaten the bark on the old apple tree. The dead parts were untouched while the golden fungus flesh was chewed on.

I hooked the crook around Goldie's neck since Blackie followed what he did and where he went. He bit on the hook. His bite was so hard I could pull him away from the tree. Blackie baaed and followed him.

Goldie let go of the shepherd's crook with a snort. He went back to the tree with the golden bough and let off a wallop of dung on its roots in spite. Blackie did the same.

"Shoo! Shoo!" I said as I chased them around the tree. I trod the dung underfoot as they ran in a determined path.

They stopped running after the roots were covered in their dung. Goldie and Blackie baaed in unison. Then they stomped away with high steps and their heads held high.

I looked at the tree in horror.

"DON'T WORRY, AMBROSIA. The dung may act as a good fertilizer," Mother said when I told her what happened at dinner.

"I swear Goldie has a mind of his own," Father said.

"Really," Mother said.

"I need to shear his fleece before it gets too long. He'll be miserable if it gets matted, but he thinks I'm playing with him when I try to catch him."

"I'm sure you'll think of something," she said.

FATHER ASSUMED IT WAS a lost cause despite Mother's encouragement. However, a day came when Goldie ran up to him.

"I don't have time to play with you now," Father said.

He bit Father's robes and pulled on them so hard it ripped the fabric. "Hey!" Goldie went on his other side and pushed him forward.

"OK. OK." He followed Goldie who led him to Blackie. He found his shepherds eating their lunch as she baaed in fear, caught in a briar bush.

"I pay you to look after my flock," Father said to Ion.

"It's not as if you can sell her wool anywhere," Ion sniffed. Father sighed. We had to keep Blackie's wool to ourselves because it couldn't be dyed. We sold a bolt occasionally when one of our neighbors was in mourning, but she didn't earn her keep.

Goldie nipped Ion so hard he drew blood. He let out a screech. "You take care of him while I get Blackie out."

I took Ion up to Mother who cleaned it his wound with wine and bandaged it with fresh linen. "It's a waste of good wine," Ion muttered.

Mother handed him the wineskin. "You can drink the rest of it to help you with the pain."

He grunted and drank it.

When Ion was taken care of I went back to Blackie. Her coat was missing chunks, but she'd been cut free. She and Goldie were nuzzling each other's muzzles while Father sheared them both. Goldie stayed still while it was done.

He glanced at Father who held the golden locks in his hand as if they were denari. Goldie nodded, then he and Blackie went off to a grassy knoll.

"Not bad wages for a day's work," Father said.

A FEW MORNINGS LATER I saw Goldie on top of Blackie! I thought the briar episode strengthened their friendship. Yet here he was crowding her like the others did.

"Oh no," I ran to Father.

"Goldie is crowding Blackie," we rushed to the pen.

Dad looked at them and said, "He isn't 'crowding' her. It's breeding season."

"Oh—I can't wait to see how their lambs turn out."

Watching their romance distracted me from my own marriage prospects. Mother said I wouldn't be married off until I stopped growing. Charis said it should be done before I got any bigger.

Menfolk preferred dryad slips and here I was growing to be a Titan. At least I'd be a comely Titan maiden thanks to Mother with her oak dryad looks. My only hope was to marry a wrestler who needed a strong woman to bear him stout sons.

We kept measuring my growth on the lintel post. Charis frowned every time she had to make another mark, "Your Father would be proud of your growth if you were a son. Hercules is the only one who won't be scared of you at this rate."

Mother shuddered at this. "I wouldn't want her to have Megara's fate!"

I bunched my hand into a fist, "At least he'd have a hard time placing his hands around my big bull neck."

I said it as a joke, but it hurt too much to laugh. It was hard to tell what to do. Was it better to marry me off when I was a marriageable size? Or was it better to spare myself the humiliation of a divorce when I became taller than my husband?

THE SHEEP DUNG REVITALIZED the golden bough so much it let off new shoots. The shoots looked like runners looking for new soil but were too far up the ground to reach it.

At least my height meant I could reach and prune the shoots. I grafted them to new roots and planted them where the first saplings had been. I then took Blackie and Goldie's dung and used it to fertilize the saplings. By the time the old tree died 12 saplings were established. They were so healthy they gave off their own radiance.

I took the apples that grew from them and pressed them into cider. When the cider fermented Mother served them to those two messengers. "This is Ambrosia's brew." I was pleased when my cider and apples became coveted. We gave them out to Iris and Mercury when they stopped by.

The day came when Mercury confirmed Charis's suspicions about him. She caught him plucking our golden apples in the orchard.

"I asked him, 'What are you doing?' and he bolted. I never saw a man move so fast," Charis reported to Mother while we sat at luncheon. Luncheon was always a simple picnic under Mother's gazebo during our workdays. She preferred to work at her weaving outside and had Father set it up for her.

Mother laughed. "He would. He's been like that since he was a baby."

"So he's of your line then?" Charis asked.

"Yes, he's my nephew."

"A scion of patricians shouldn't act like a thieving peasant," Charis sniffed.

"Maybe he thought the apples were actually gold? If that's the case, he'll be disappointed," I said.

Mother sighed, "Oh, he's well aware of their value. That's why he took them without asking. He didn't think we'd give them to him if he asked for them."

"So the Golden Bough apples are rare?" I asked.

Mother nodded. "There's only one other garden that grows them, and the apples are well guarded there."

Her comment made me assume the Golden Boughs were a rare variety, and I did what it took to take care of my orchard.

THE BIRTH OF BLACKIE and Goldie's lamb gave us a reason to praise the gods for our good fortune. Nugget had his mother's black face and his father's coat which meant yet more golden fleece for us.

Mother wove a cloak from Goldie's wool. It was so shiny when it was done Father said, "Best to give it as an offering to Jupiter. It's too ostentatious for anyone else!"

I expected her to send it to the Temple, but she gave it to Iris who said, "I'll see it reaches him."

Father invited the Arcadian's temple priest to sacrifice an offering. They sent back a perfectly good ram.

"What's wrong with it?" he said, wondering if he'd missed a flaw in his chosen sacrifice. It was a white ram without spot. I couldn't see how the temple could ask for more.

"Give us the golden fleece," the temple guard said.

"What?"

"Your good fortune is giving you too much hubris. Such a fine animal belongs only to the gods," he said.

Mother was spinning the wool in the gazebo. Most times she ignored the men's conversation. Now she straightened herself to her full height with her distaff full of golden thread. "Yes, the golden fleece belongs to the gods."

"And a vestal virgin is just as good a mediator as Apollo's priest," Father said.

The guard took one look at me, who was obviously their child and said, "She isn't a vestal virgin anymore."

"I served my term," Mother snapped.

"It's best to cull the golden fleece before he becomes too dangerous. Medea's father gave his to the Colchis temple when it developed bloodlust."

"Apollo, will have to get the golden fleece himself if he wants it. His mediators shouldn't ask for more than a good white ram," Father said...

His comment caused a scandal that even Iris heard of. "Your field-hand has gotten presumptuous if he hoards a gift that belongs to the gods."

Mother frowned, "Field-hand?"

"The one who tends the golden fleece."

"Ambrose is my husband," Mother said.

I was present, and Iris glanced at me. "Ambrosia is our daughter."

Iris's mouth dropped open as if Mother was still in active service at the shrine, and she'd broken her vows. "But you rejected Venus's gifts."

"Venus has horrible taste in men. Why would I accept the recommendations of a woman who welcomes Mars into her bed?" Mother waved her hand. "She proved her lack of good sense by inviting Silenus to Cybele's party on a blind date. Then she induced me to sample Dionysus's latest vintage."

Iris fell silent for a long moment before saying, "But you rejected Neptune and Apollo's suits. You took a vow of perpetual chastity."

"What I said is, 'I'd rather be a virgin then settle for Venus's offerings.' I never said I'd never choose for myself."

THE NEXT DAY A LORD appeared at our gate while we ate our breakfast in Mother's gazebo. He was so grand he could've been the Roman Emperor. I gaped at the sight of the cloak Mother had woven from Goldie's wool on his shoulders and realized who this man must be.

Jupiter glared at Father. "This is the man who dares to desecrate a virgin goddess? I've come here to punish your hubris myself."

Mother merely gave a nod of the head, and said, "Jupiter," to confirm my guess

Father gasped.

"Why have you broken your vow, Vesta?"

"I abdicated my position in Olympus after Silenus tried to dishonor me," she shrugged. "I hear Dionysus has my position in the pantheon and is doing well."

"This union isn't valid unless he shows an ability to provide for you in a manner befitting a goddess."

"He's on the verge of providing me a flock of golden fleece now that he's found a mate for Goldie. He's given me Ambrosia. Olympus drinks her cider since the apples of youth are withheld from them now. They have more to offer Olympus than that pretty-boy you made your cupbearer."

"Humph," Jupiter waved his hand toward Nugget who was grazing in a field. A spark of lightning went off in his direction. Nugget baaed in annoyance. His wool stood on end before the bolt got channeled into the ground. A black circle of scorched earth appeared around him.

"Hm, he takes after his sire. That'll mean his wool is fireproof," Jupiter said.

Mother sighed. "As you can see my husband and daughter's labor have built up my estate. Each of Cronus's children were given a golden bough from Hesperides's garden. We each got a golden lamb from Helios's flock by right of conquest when we defeated the Titans. You have no right to my share of the booty if I wish to use it as a dowry."

His eyes narrowed, "I knew only of the lamb. Why do you speak of the golden bough?"

Just our luck the clouds in the sky parted to cast a sunbeam on our orchard of trees. He gasped as the trees glowed golden and Mother groaned.

His eyes narrowed.

"You've got Ceres at Mt. Olympus, Brother. Don't tell me she hasn't figured out how to transplant the Golden Boughs," Mother said.

Lightning flashed and thunder rolled in response." We've all been eating one apple a century and awaiting our demise from old age. You've been toasting your health with cider pressed from the golden bough apples.

We ate and skinned Helios's golden sheep when they were too unmanageable. You've been raising a flock and weaving golden cloaks with their wool."

He took a deep breath and made a new demand:

"Ambrose must start a herd of golden fleece for Mount Olympus. Ambrosia must set up a grove of Golden Boughs capable of producing nectar worthy of the gods." Jupiter grumbled and thunder rumbled in the distance at his words.

"So be it," Father said. "But I'm not a god. I can't do the work by myself. Let me bring my household with me."

Lightning flashed while Mother sighed, "Do you want me married to a poor provider, Brother? Ambrose's servants are honest, hardworking folk who contribute to the civic order."

OLYMPUS'S FIRST AMBROSIAN Mystery was a taste test of the hard cider I made from the golden bough apples. The gods found themselves reinvigorated by the ambrosia. This caused Minerva to declare the details of ambrosia's manufacture a state secret. We allowed our servants a taste as a part of their wages. Thus, the Arcadians became a part of the Ambrosian Mysteries too.

The gods' state secrets are "mysteries" no matter how prosaic they are.

Father and I partake of the ambrosia though no one knows of our existence outside of Mt. Olympus. Mortals assume Vesta is an eternal virgin. The only hint of her family's existence are the references to "ambrosia, the food of the gods". I'm the only demigod Juno views favorably because, "She earns her keep."

Nemesis can't believe that a mortal desecrated a virgin goddess with no penalty. She would've struck Father down to the lowest pit to Tartarus for such hubris if she had her way. Instead, she has to tell herself that eternal farm labor in Olympus is punishment enough.

No one talks of turning Father into a grasshopper. Nor doubts his usefulness. He tends the flock of bloodthirsty golden sheep, that even Mars is leery of. He's an Olympian by marriage. The ambrosia keeps him healthy and hardy. The fact he isn't an Adonis means Mother keeps him to herself. He's so prosaic neither Venus nor the other goddesses envy Mother. Mother says he should be a god of husbandry for all his hard work, but Jupiter won't allow it. He renamed Father "Ambrose Sanctus" but that's the only concession he's willing to make.

The goddesses may've allowed Mother to keep her husband in peace, but envied her field-hands:

"I may be the Goddess of Agriculture, but do you think I want to tend my fields myself? Why can't I have field-hands willing to do menial work too!" Ceres demanded at one of their councils.

This made a swell of complaints crest:

"There'd be more wine in Olympus if I could find men to work my vineyard. I can only supply so much wine when I'm dependent on my followers' drink offerings," Dionysus said.

"I drive a fiery chariot every day," Apollo muttered. "I want a flock of golden sheep that grow fireproof wool too."

Jupiter gave the job of finding help for farm-work to Father.

Father had to use his contacts to fill the position. The Olympians look for good help and laborers in Arcadia. This inspired the pastoral poetry that glorifies rural life among Roman writers. We appreciate their contributions. Yet the gods don't want it known common laborers can ascend to Olympus. Most heroes only make it to the Isle of the Blest but they want to stop laboring then.

Thus, the great secret of the Ambrosian Mysteries is that it is an Olympian hiring fair. Followers get screened for jobs. Some see working in Olympus as the ultimate act of devotion. Others only see it as a job even if it's got the best benefits a farm laborer can hope for.

Acolytes uninterested in working don't ascend to Olympus: "There's people who'd think Mt. Olympus was Tartarus if they knew they'd have to work for their keep." Charis mutters when she sees a lazy newcomer in Arcadia.

The last time Charis mentioned marriage was after my latest growth spurt. "You must marry a Titan if you marry at all, girl."

The ambrosia cider means I can afford to wait. I'm not sure if I plan to take up Mother's vow of chastity, but the option is still available so far...

So, now I've recorded all the details about ambrosia. It deserves a more epic treatment than I've given it, but I'm no Homer or Virgil. I don't have the talent to make an Iliad or Aeneid. Maybe the Muses can turn the notes in this scroll into an inspiration for the artists they favor. The members of the Ambrosian Mysteries and I are too busy to compose hymns and write epics.

# The Weft and Warp of Hubris

ARES'S FEASTS WERE mandatory for Athena. They weren't always to her taste, but she came because she was one of the Olympian war gods. He often mounted them to commemorate great battles. One war god should've been enough, but they would've lost the War of the Titans without her.

She didn't deny Ares was a greater warrior than her. It was too bad he was too impulsive to form coherent strategies. They would've won battles but lost the war with the Titans if not for her tactics. That's why the Olympians divided the labor between them. Ares was in charge of feats of martial valor while she inspired the strategy and tactics needed to win wars.

No one thought of her and Ares as a team, but they worked as such for the sake of Olympus's security. Ares wouldn't do that much if he didn't find the strategy sessions boring. He preferred the battlefield over the war room. That's why he offloaded the strategy sessions to her. Otherwise, Athena would only be the Goddess of Weaving.

Much to her surprise Ares had a tapestry instead of a war trophy on display at this latest banquet. It showed Ares and Aphrodite entrapped by the love goddess's jealous husband Hephaestus. The two were encased in a fine mesh that did nothing to hide their nudity. Vibrant colors in the piece reflected their divine vitality.

Aphrodite shrieked at the sight of it, but not in shame. "Is this a sign you'll break your vow of chastity soon?"

The archness of her tone made Athena flush in anger. "Why should I break my vow now? I saw you two together already and didn't care less."

Hephaestus had invited all Olympus to witness the spectacle when it happened. Athena got tricked into coming when she thought he was exhibiting an invention.

Aphrodite's brows rose. "Yet, you weaved this tapestry."

"No, I didn't," Athena declared.

Aphrodite gestured to the skill displayed in the weaving of the tapestry. "Come on! Who else could've done this?"

"I weave war banners for Ares's favored general and memorials of his battles." Athena gestured to one of him wielding a blazing sword against a Titan.

"Not his conquests," she emphasized the last by pointing to the real and depicted Aphrodite.

"Hm," Venus touched the fabric of the tapestry. She chose a section that showed Ares and stroked it in much the same way as when she stroked his flesh.

"This weaver is a great artist. They have as much skill as you even if they take on commissions you refuse."

She grinned, "I have half a mind to commission a piece to commemorate my first step onto Cyprus."

Athena snorted at this. Venus was born when Cronus's "foam" was cast into the ocean. She then floated on a seashell to the island.

Nemesis came to the tapestry. "She's good. It's a pity I must strike her down. 'Arachne' even had the gall to sign her work."

Ares and Aphrodite frowned, "Why?"

"She's showing you both in a bad light."

Aphrodite laughed. "More like in our glory. That's not offensive!"

"Very well, Arachne is not charged with hubris," Nemesis nodded before she wandered off.

"Well she better not show ME in such a state," Artemis said.

Athena sniffed, "What do I care if this Arachne caters to the exhibitionists."

Eris snickered, "The Aegean sculptors sculpt the gods naked."

Athena frowned, "I know my images have robes."

"The goddesses do, except for Aphrodite. Zeus and the other gods think of the nude statues as advertising."

Hera rolled her eyes at this, "What do you expect from men?"

Athena snorted agreement.

THE WEAVER LEFT ATHENA'S mind when she discovered Athens was constructing the Parthenon. It'd be a grand temple in honor of all the Olympians where each of them would have a niche. Its design was so grand that Athena planned to weave a tapestry for it.

She spent days weaving it, keeping it a secret before its unveiling.

Zeus went down to inspect the Parthenon. He came back praising it. "It's grand in every detail, but I love Athena's tapestry most of all."

"My tapestry? I haven't finished it yet."

"Well the one on the wall depicted the time when you all tried to use Hephaestus's chains to bind me. It was the ultimate moment of greatness for me. This tapestry captures it perfectly!" Zeus smiled.

The other Olympians frowned at this. However, Eris, the Goddess of Discord, smiled, "Why don't we all check this tapestry out?"

ATHENA JOINED THE GROUP in the guise of Mentor. Everyone else disguised themselves as mortals but chose to be noble dignitaries.

Eris laughed while everyone else scowled at the sight of Zeus's glory outshining them all.

"Glorious isn't it?" Zeus said.

No one dared say anything.

Eris touched the fabric, "Look the artist wove their name into the tapestry! It's Arachne again."

Ares nodded at this. "She seems intent on giving each of us a fitting tapestry. This time it was Zeus's turn."

Eris looked Athena square in the eye. "I can't wait for my turn."

"Did the rest of us get tapestries?" She went to the spot where Athena, Hera and Aphrodite statues were clustered. Eris gasped in true delight. A banner showed her on the opposite wall presenting them a golden apple with a knowing smirk. The men chuckled at this.

"I love it," Eris cried out. She reached out to pull the tapestry down.

Hermes's brows rose, "I thought I was the God of Thieves, not you Eris?"

"This is our temple. Everything that's in here belongs to the Olympians. Taking a tapestry, I like to my palace in Olympus isn't petty theft it's an honor," Eris pouted.

"This is ridiculous." Athena muttered.

Zeus glanced at his own tapestry, "She has a point. I'd like to take mine with me too."

THE MISSING TAPESTRIES got taken as a sign of divine displeasure. All work on the Parthenon stopped, and augers sought to appease the gods. Zeus responded with a shower of gold "to put towards the Temple," to clear the misunderstanding.

Eris added a bowl full of golden apples for the best tapestry woven for the temple. Her generosity shocked the Olympians, "I want to see what Arachne comes up with when she has incentive."

Athena had her own ideas.

SHE WANTED TO GIVE the mortals a glimpse of Olympus's sacred halls. Her composition was of the gods' symposium, which was far grander than any on Earth.

Her submission to the contest was hand-delivered, and the priest smiled, "It'll be a tough call."

"Tough call," she screeched like the crone she looked like.

"You and Arachne are on the short list," the priest said.

"Short list? Short list?" She should've been the clear-cut winner!

ATHENA CAME BACK ON the day of the final announcement for the contest. She looked like a crone with her back crooked by work over the loom.

It was all she could do not to snicker at the sight of Arachne. The woman was squat and stumpy with her back already humped from her loom. At least she could cast aside this crone's body anytime she wanted.

"It was a tough call, but we've narrowed the field down to two finalists," The priest said.

"Pallas of Athens," the townspeople cheered in a show of hometown loyalty. Athena took it as her due from her patron city.

"Arachne of Hypæpæ," brought about raucous cheers from a matron in the crowd with heavy makeup and a saucy tilt to her chin. Arachne smiled at the audience's applause.

Both of their tapestries were framed on the wall behind drapes.

"This is Pallas's entry," people clapped at the sight of the Olympic Symposium.

"Excellent, we should exhibit this in the symposium," a patrician man murmured.

"And here is Arachne's," there was a moment of stunned silence at the sight of a Dionysian feast in Olympus's halls. Side panels showed the gods in siderooms engaged in various indiscretions.

That matron squealed in delight. "I want this in my boudoir."

Everyone else broke out in laughter and applause, and Athena saw red. She lashed out at Arachne's tapestry with a bronze knife.

"Stop her! Stop her!"

She threw off the guards and her crone guise in one instant. They cowered before her in her rage and glory. A hush fell over most of the audience, but that matron dared to scream, "NO!" when Athena wrapped a thick chord around Arachne's neck. She suspended Arachne from the rafters as a warning against hubris.

She smirked as Arachne's face turned purple. "I charge you with hubris, Mortal. You are hanging now and will hang in Tartarus.

She disappeared in a flash of light that the priest worried would cause a fire. He and the judges rushed out except for that matron who gaped at Arachne. Tears pooled in her eyes and left black streaks down her cheeks from her kohl makeup.

The lines on her face smoothed out as she spoke. "I didn't have the power to stop Athena, but I can save you from Tartarus, Arachne. I Eris, Goddess of Discord, dare to say the things others refuse to say in Olympus and I admire your handiwork. You are the best of weavers and I will grant you a form that allows you to continue to weave."

She took out a herb from her a pouch and threw it in Arachne's direction. The weight on Arachne's throat lightened. She pushed at the noose with her hands and found she had more than two. Once she was free of the noose, she spun a line from her belly and anchored it to the ground.

Arachne realized she was a spider the size of a lapdog. She landed next to Eris, "Athena's wrath insists on a punishment. That's why I used Hecate's herbs to change you, but you'll have an honored place in my household."

IT TOOK A WHILE TO adjust, but Arachne had never been a beauty and Eris's household accepted her presence. Besides that, she had her work for solace. Eris's tales of Olympian misdemeanors and exploits inspired new tapestries.

Arachne's first work was a panel that showed Athena's face red with rage when she showed up in Olympus! Athena could do nothing when Zeus deemed Arachne's spider form punishment enough. "I decree it so as payment for my favorite banner."

# The Midas Metamorphoses

MIDAS WON THE GODS' favor with his wisdom. He was so outstanding they invited him to an Olympian feast and agreed to give him anything he desired. Midas's love of gold often blinded his better judgment despite his wisdom. He could've asked for his weight in gold, and he would've gotten it. They would've even given him a room full of gold, but not even this was enough for him. His lust for gold was such an unquenchable fire he said, "I wish to be surrounded by gold all of my life."

Apollo looked at him with raised brows. Nemesis's eyes narrowed, and she said, "Let me be the one to give Midas his heart's desire."

These requests surprised the gods, but they granted them.

Midas assumed the gods would give him his gift then, but instead he was sent away with his head full of wine. The wine was superb, and Midas drank all the toasts the gods made to him. He fell into a deep slumber that night. When he awoke, he was in a bed of gold!

This meant that Nemesis turned him into a dragon because of his greed. She meant this as a punishment, a crucible from which he'd cry for mercy, but Midas considered it a well-earned reward. He saw his bulk as a means to protect his treasures and his ability to breathe fire as a way to smelt his hoard. Midas was so grateful he commissioned a temple be built in Nemesis's honor.

This shocked Nemesis, but Apollo told her, "At least you taught Midas proper respect for the gods."

# Scorned by Narcissus

THIS LAMENT FROM A scorned lover came to Nemesis along acrid fumes one day. It was written in elegant yet sharp pen strokes as if they were etched on the parchment with bile. She unrolled it with great anticipation, and it didn't disappoint her.

ODE TO NARCISSUS

It was love at first sight when I first saw you, but you were already taken.

I thought you were looking into my eyes, but you saw no deeper than your own reflection.

If you want to be Narcissus,

Then I'll be Nemesis,

And carry you down to Tartarus!

I thought I could steal you from your latest

I didn't know you already considered yourself the greatest

And I couldn't compete with that!

If you want to be Narcissus,

Then I'll be Nemesis,

And carry you down to Tartarus!

I was content to worship the ground you walked on

But I didn't realize your Triple Gods were Me, Myself and I!

So now I want to be an iconoclast instead of a worshiper at the shrine.

Because if you want to be Narcissus,

Then I'll be Nemesis,

And carry you down to Tartarus!

So, go ahead and stare into that pool

I'll drag you down and hold you under

So, I can make you drown in your own reflection
You won't be able to float away without a care in the world this time
Because if you want to be Narcissus,
Then I'll be Nemesis,
And carry you down to Tartarus!

*Nemesis chuckled at such eloquent fury. She fingered an arrow from Cupid as she contemplated her response. You shall not only see your Narcissus humbled. You shall also taste the favors you crave.*

*PLEASE LEAVE A REVIEW if you enjoyed seeing Nemesis's work overruled. You can sign up for my mailing list at bit.ly/2dfusEh so you'll know when my next release comes out.*

# About the Author

CATHY SMITH IS A MOHAWK writer who lives on a Status Reservation on the Canadian Side of the Border.

She is proud of her people's heritage, and has an interest in the traditions of other cultures. Most of her works to date have been based on the folkloric traditions she's studied. Science fiction and fantasy strikes her as the folklore of the modern age and she considers both genres a natural choice for her own writings.

You can also follow her at:

Twitter: @khiatons

Facebook: bit.ly/2dP3rXd

Wordpress: bit.ly/2e41qWT

Pinterest: bit.ly/2fGMgqP

Instagram: cathy2891

Tumblr: bit.ly/2G3dEjo

Tiktok: bit.ly/3KoGwBf

Sign up to the Cathy Smith-Khiatons-I Write Substack https://bit.ly/4qATMGH to receive news and excerpts of new publications and promotions.

www.ingramcontent.com/pod-product-compliance
Lightning Source LLC
Chambersburg PA
CBHW051419130726
47989CB00007B/2997